Praise for
New York Times bestselling author
Sharon Page

"Sharon Page shines with this riveting tale of true love...
The rip-roaring plot kept me turning pages far into the night."
—*New York Times* bestselling author Sabrina Jeffries on
An American Duchess

"Fans of *Downton Abbey* should reach for *An American Duchess*...
Page's captivating prose evokes the Roaring Twenties with skillful
and vivid details and creates a searing romance with a timeless
message."
—International bestselling author Pam Jenoff

"Merging the flavor of *Downton Abbey* with her own special
touches, Page crafts a vibrant novel and a dramatic love story [that]
completely captures the angst and glamour of the era."
—*RT Book Reviews* on *An American Duchess*

"With danger and erotic intrigue at every turn, *The Club* is a fast
paced, blistering page turner that evokes the emotional and erotic
with every scene."
—*USA TODAY* bestselling author Kathryn Smith

"A winner."
—*Publishers Weekly*, starred review, on *The Club*

"[A]n intensely emotional love story. It isn't only the sizzle that rivets
readers, it's the true passion and love that [Page] infuses into the
story that makes it a deep-sigh read."
—*RT Book Reviews* on *Engaged in Sin* (Top Pick)

"Anticipation...smolders on every page."
—*RT Book Reviews* on

THE
WORTHINGTON
WIFE

SHARON PAGE

HQN™

Recycling programs
for this product may
not exist in your area.

ISBN-13: 978-0-373-78854-5

The Worthington Wife

Copyright © 2016 by Edith E. Bruce

This edition published by arrangement with Harlequin Books S.A.

For questions and comments about the quality of this book, please contact us
at CustomerService@Harlequin.com.

® and TM are trademarks of Harlequin Enterprises Limited or its corporate affiliates.
Trademarks indicated with ® are registered in the United States Patent and
Trademark Office, the Canadian Intellectual Property Office and in other countries.

www.HQNBooks.com

Printed in U.S.A.

THE
WORTHINGTON
WIFE

1

The American Heir

"I don't *care* about scandal, Nigel." Lady Julia Hazelton marched up to the desk in the study of her brother, the Duke of Langford, and set her palms on the smooth oak edge. "These women lost their husbands to war and now there is *nothing* for them. If they have farms or stores or homes, they are being turned out of them, despite having children to feed and clothe. I can help them. What do you think I will do? Do you really think I'll be inspired, after spending time with a fallen woman, to stand outside the village public house, plying the trade?"

"Good God, Julia!" Her brother, startlingly handsome with raven-black hair and brilliant blue eyes, jolted in his chair. Fortunately he had a secure grip on the very precious bundle he held. Nigel wore his tweeds, but a lacy blanket hung over his shoulder. Napping on his shoulder was his eleven-month-old son, holding his father's strong hands.

Nigel blushed scarlet. "The fact you know so much about such things speaks for itself."

"I thought Zoe finally cured you of your stuffiness, Nigel," Julia said.

Zoe was her brother's American bride, the "American Duchess" famous in the British newspapers—once famous for her wild style of living, now famous for her brilliance in investing and in turning Brideswell into the most modern yet beautiful house in England.

Cradling his son, Nigel said, "Julia, I agree that the plight of the war widows is terrible. But the responsibility for it doesn't rest on your shoulders. You have been loaning money to them out of your pin money—"

"What I am supposed to do? Simply pretend I don't see the women who look as if they've lost their souls, because they are hoping some man gives them a few pennies to—to poke at them?"

"Julia! Where, for the love of God, did you learn expressions like that?"

"Nigel, there was a war on. I'm afraid that one of the casualties of war is innocence. You were there. You know how brave those men were, and how wrong it is that they are dead."

"I know that. As a result, Zoe and I have given to many charities—"

"But once these women sell themselves, they don't go to charities for help. Some of these women were left alone, with babies even younger than Nicholas. I would go to terrible lengths if my child was starving."

"Yes, but—"

"These women do not have a choice. With money, they would!"

"Yes, but—"

"Many of them have skills—they have run households and farms."

"Yes, but—"

"They could start businesses. They could better themselves. They could give futures to their children."

This time her brother didn't bother with a *yes, but.*

"Julia, this work is not helping your marriage prospects."

"Oh, *that's* what you all are worried about."

Now that Zoe and Nigel were married and Julia's dowry was restored—from the investments made from Zoe's fortune—her brother, her mother and her grandmother wanted to see her wed.

"I've lost two men that I loved, Nigel. I lost Anthony to the Battle of the Somme. And Dougal to the idiocy of our class system. Frankly, I've given up on getting married."

Nigel shifted his son in his arms. "Don't, Julia."

"Well, I have." Julia crossed her arms over her chest defiantly. "But I can still do something *worthwhile.* I have the power to help these women. No bank would loan them money. But—"

She knew people thought her to be a cool, controlled, reserved English lady, but there were times when her heart hammered passionately and she was willing to fight to the ends of the earth if she had to. Two years ago, accompanied by her American sister-in-law, Zoe, Julia had begun to be daring. She had put mourning behind her and taken risks, only to have her heart broken again, this time by the brilliant Dr. Dougal Campbell, who believed they could never bridge the divide between their positions. She'd retreated back into the world she knew. She'd hidden all her emotion behind ladylike behavior.

Until now. Last week, she had seen a woman named Ellen Lambert struck by a brute of a man on the village street.

The man had run when Julia approached, waving her umbrella and shouting for help. She'd learned Ellen's story and Julia had seen, with horror, how insulated her life had been.

"But?" Nigel prompted.

"But *I* would. I want a loan against my dowry, Nigel. I can use that to provide money to widows like Ellen Lambert of the village. They can pay it back over a reasonable time and with a reasonable interest."

"Julia, your dowry is there—"

"To bribe men to marry me."

"That is not true. For a start, no man would need a bribe to propose to you."

"Really? No gentleman looked at me twice when the estate was close to bankruptcy and I didn't have the dowry."

Nicholas stirred. Nigel ran his large hand over the baby's small back, gently soothing. "That had nothing to do with it. Everyone knew you were still grieving Anthony and you weren't ready to move on."

Oh, how Julia's heart gave a pang as her brother stroked his son. Without marriage, she would never have such a moment with a child of her own.

Was it worth marrying a man she didn't love to have a child she could love?

Once she would have emphatically said no. Now, with adorable baby Nicholas in the house, a strange madness would sometimes overtake her. She had to *fight* the dangerous idea that marriage without love could somehow work. She knew it didn't. She knew that from living with unhappily married parents.

And she didn't believe she could ever fall in love again. She had been in love twice—she'd lost Anthony to war, and Dr. Campbell when he'd left her to go to the London Hospital. Her heart had been broken twice. She didn't think she could survive a third time.

Nigel looked up from his infant son. "Julia, promise you will not give up on the idea of marriage."

"Nigel, I—" She broke off. Suspicion grew at the hopeful look in her brother's blue eyes. "Oh no. Say you didn't—"

"Did not what?" he asked innocently.

"You didn't invite a prospective husband to the house... again?"

"No, no. We are dining at Worthington Park tonight. But a friend of mine is going to be there. A friend from Oxford. An admirable chap. He's now the Earl of Summerhay."

"Nigel, I am not exactly out of love with Dougal yet." She had just received a rather devastating letter from Dougal, but this would give her an excuse. "I am definitely not ready to fall in love with anyone else." That was certainly true. She didn't even think it could ever be possible.

Her brother lifted an autocratic brow. "Dr. Campbell did a sensible thing. You couldn't be a doctor's wife. You should be running a house like Brideswell."

"I think I would have been very happy as a doctor's wife." True, but it was pointless now, wasn't it? "But Dougal believed we could not circumvent the difference in our social positions." In fact, like her brother, Dougal thought she needed a grand estate and a title. "Grandmama and Mother worked at Dougal until he went away to London. Honestly, I wouldn't be surprised if Grandmama paid a gamekeeper to escort Dougal to the train station with a rifle at his back."

"She wants you to be happy."

"No, she does not if her only objection was that she didn't want her oldest granddaughter married to a mere doctor. But Dougal has saved lives. I don't want an earl or a duke. I've realized that I want a hero. When I saw what Dougal could do, I was struck with awe."

Nigel frowned. "But I do not think Dr. Campbell is worthy of you. He should have stayed and fought for you. You are worthy of a dragon slayer. Your doctor may have saved lives, but I don't know if he has enough courage for you, Julia."

"Is your earl a dragon slayer?"

She was surprised by how serious Nigel suddenly looked. "I know what he did in the War, Julia. I think he is."

"So you won't give me my loan?"

"I cannot distract you, can I?"

"No."

He sighed. "I want to see you happily settled, Julia. So my answer has to be no."

She could argue. And fight. Or she could be smart about this. "I will ask Zoe for a loan."

"In this, Zoe will not disagree with me."

"Maybe not. But I can at least try." She turned and walked away.

"Julia."

She paused at the door.

"Summerhay will not be the only eligible man there. Lady Worthington has invited the Duke of Bradstock, my friend from Eton days. Along with Viscount Yorkville. Three intelligent, interesting men."

James, the duke, she knew quite well. One of his many houses was only an hour away by motorcar, and he would visit on school holidays. He had been born to be a duke—he could be rather arrogant. Yorkville, she'd never met.

"Nigel, you can't push me at eligible men at Worthington Park." She sighed. "It's bad form when Lady Carstairs will want to do that with *her* three unmarried daughters."

"Julia, all I am asking you to do is be polite," her brother protested.

"That is all anyone wants me to do. Be polite and lady-like and boring. But I am not giving up."

Then she swept out of his study. But it was not such a dramatic exit—she was leaving to do what was expected of her. To dress for dinner.

But she longed to burst out of her shell. To do something that was more than just wild and frivolous, like dancing and drinking cocktails.

Her sister-in-law, Zoe, could fly airplanes. There were women doctors, singers, artists, clothing designers. A modern woman could now grasp almost any opportunity, take hold of life and become something.

Modern women could change the world. That was what she wanted to do.

That night, the Daimler took Julia, her mother, sister Isobel and grandmother to Worthington Park. Zoe and Nigel followed in Zoe's sporty motor.

The car door was opened by one of Worthington's footmen. A warm early-summer breeze flirted with the gauzy, bead-strewn hem of her skirt as Julia stepped out on the drive and gazed up at the house that might have been her home.

Brideswell Abbey, the house she'd grown up in, was more square and severe. Worthington was sprawling and inviting. It had a long facade, with two wings that came forward like embracing arms. A massive fountain stood in the middle of the circular drive. In the June sun, the house glowed with warm golden stone and hundreds of windows glinted.

With Mother and Grandmama, Julia walked into the foyer. Her heels clicked on the black marble tiles, the sound soaring to the high domed ceiling and its exquisite art, gilded with gold leaf. The newel post and railing of the stairs gleamed with gilt and the walls were covered partway in white and rose-pink marble. Orchids from the greenhouses and roses spilled out of enormous vases.

Julia handed off her wrap to a footman.

It was in here, in the very open foyer, that Anthony had stolen his first kiss. She had been unwinding her scarf while the butler fetched Anthony's sister Diana, who was Julia's age and a good friend. From behind, Anthony had swept her into his arms. At the soft, wonderful caress of his lips on hers, her heart had raced and she'd almost melted. Then he'd heard the butler returning, so he'd let her go and run off. But he'd thrown her one last look—a look of pure, hungry, masculine longing that had seared her to her toes.

Two days later, he'd proposed to her.

They had walked to the folly—a temple with white marble columns that stood on a hill and overlooked the house. It had been a rainy, windswept day, but they'd had so few days before Anthony would be leaving for France and war.

She had been not quite eighteen. For a year, since she had come out, everyone expected she would marry Anthony. But she had still been young and there had been time. Then war had come, and suddenly everyone was afraid there would not be time anymore—not enough time to live.

Anthony had said, "Someday I will be the Earl of Worthington but none of that matters if you aren't with me. Don't say we're too young. I'm old enough to go and fight and I want to know things are settled between us before I go. I love you, Julia. I wish I could marry you before I leave, but I should be back soon, and we'll be married then."

"We will," she had said. "I love you." Then he'd swept her into his arms and kissed her again…

Anthony had died at the Somme in 1916.

Julia let out a long soft breath as she, her mother and grandmother walked toward the drawing room. Worthington Park was special to her. For her, it was filled with the happiness and the excitement of her very first love. It was wrapped up in loss, too.

Even running her hand along a banister or taking a seat in a chair gave her a powerful, electrifying jolt of memory and emotion.

"Julia!"

Her friend Diana came forward, her golden hair bouncing around her lovely face. Her huge blue eyes gave her a helpless look, but her painted Cupid's bow lips and pencil-straight sheath of gold beads and lace were thoroughly modern.

Julia knew Diana fought a constant battle with her mother, Lady Worthington, over her shocking use of makeup, but because she bought her cosmetics from the counter at Selfridges, not because makeup was scandalous anymore.

Diana clasped her hands. "Come with me and we'll have a smart cocktail instead of the horrid sweet sherry my mother insists on. I must talk to you!"

Julia followed Diana to one of the bay windows that looked out upon the side lawns. Worthington Park had one of the most ordered gardens in the country. Behind the house, paths followed a delicate design leading through beds to a central fountain.

A footman brought a silver tray with two enormous glasses, truly the size of finger bowls. Bubbles floated up through the liquid, which was tinted pink.

"Champagne cocktails," Diana said. She took several long swallows.

"Diana—" Julia frowned. "You should slow down." Diana had been drinking much too much of late. They had been in London together last week and she'd rescued a drunken

Diana from a party and taken her to the Savoy to keep Diana from getting behind the wheel and driving when she could barely stand.

"It's for courage," Diana protested. "They found the heir and he's coming here to see exactly what he's inherited—what he gets to take away from us."

Diana's ominous words made Julia shiver. The heir to Worthington had been found. After the old earl had died at the end of the War, Anthony's younger brother, John, had inherited the title. Tragically, John Carstairs had died a year ago in a car crash and the hunt had begun for the next in line to the title.

"What do you mean, what he gets to take away from you?"

"Mummy believes this man—who's American—will turn us out to starve. He hates us all."

"For heaven's sake, why?"

Diana drained her cocktail. "It's all very thrilling. His mother was Irish, a maid working in a house in New York City. My grandmother disowned her younger son—my uncle—over the marriage and the family cut off all ties. It left them in poverty. So Mummy fears he will throw us out into poverty now."

"Surely your mother is wrong. That was years ago, and it was not your fault. This man can't still be bitter and mean to be so harsh." Now Julia saw how pale her friend was beneath her rouge. She was truly afraid. "Diana, it would be ridiculous. After a World War, this man must see that family feuds are utterly meaningless. He must have a decent nature that can be appealed to."

"Mummy doesn't think so. And to protect us, Mummy wants me to marry him. He is my cousin, but royal cousins marry all the time, including first cousins. It would all be quite legal."

"This is 1925. No one will force you to marry, Diana, against your will."

Diana laughed a cold, jaded laugh that sent another chill down Julia's spine. "The thing is—I am willing to marry him. By all reports, he's quite handsome. He's going to be an earl. Master of my home. If one of my brothers had become the earl, I would have had to marry to survive. It's what women like us have to do. And this way I can have everything—a rather sexy husband, the title of countess and the home I grew up in."

How strong were these cocktails? "But you haven't even met this man. Don't let your mother push you into something ill-advised."

"I've decided that I really must have a husband. And there are so few men left for us. The War took them from us." Suddenly Diana grasped her forearm. "I need you to help me, Julia. He's arriving in time for dinner, then he's going to stay. I must convince him to propose."

Julia looked at Diana's worried face and huge blue eyes. "I suspect he will fall in love with you the first moment he sees you."

"He won't. He really does hate us because the family cut his father off. Apparently, this Cal holds rather a grudge. He doesn't even use his real name. That's why it took so long to find him. He goes by his mother's maiden name of Brody."

The footman came past and Diana snatched another cocktail. "I think convincing him to marry me might prove a challenge. Because, you see, I have to convince him to like me."

"Why shouldn't he like you?"

"Because...well, isn't it obvious? He will see me as the privileged daughter who had everything while his family lived in squalor. I need to be more like you, Julia. Doing

good works and such. Mummy is going to try every trick
in the book to force a marriage, but her ideas will be crude
and obvious. They will be the kind of plots intended to work
on Englishmen with a sense of honor and obligation. I don't
think that's going to work on an angry American."

"I don't understand what you mean."

Diana waved her hand and champagne sloshed over the
glass. "Oh, Mummy would think that if the American was
found in my bedroom, he would feel he had to marry me.
She's dreadfully Victorian when it comes to scheming. My
plan is to be the sort of woman he can admire. Of course I
have no idea what sort of woman that is. Maybe it isn't the
noble saint. Maybe he would like a bad girl. You observe
people and understand them. Figure out the kind of woman
he wants and help me to convince him I'm that woman."

"Diana, this is mad. How can you possibly want to marry
a man you do not know—" *and apparently fear* "—based on
trying to be someone you are not?"

The Countess of Worthington was approaching and Diana
put her lips right beside Julia's ear. "Darling, I'm pregnant,"
she whispered. "I have to marry. I *have* to."

Pregnant? Julia floundered to think of something to say,
but Diana looked to the door and said, in husky tones, "Oh
Lord, it's the American. He's arrived."

The butler, Wiggins, looked as if he'd sucked on a lemon,
but he cleared his throat, gave a glance of complete disdain at the astonishing-looking man beside him—he had to
look up to do it—and announced, "His lordship, the Earl
of Worthington."

"It's Cal," the man said. A slow, wicked grin curved his
mouth as if he was enjoying himself immensely.

"Oh, good heavens," the countess moaned quietly. "He
looks like he was found in a ditch. *How* can this man be the

earl instead of my sons?" Unsteady suddenly, she almost fell over. Julia hastened to the countess's side and supported her.

The man who called himself Cal stood well over six feet tall. A threadbare blue sweater stretched across his chest, topped by a worn and faded leather coat. He wore a laborer's rough trousers. His black boots had never seen a lick of polish.

His tanned face set off his golden hair, which was slicked back with pomade, but light, shimmering strands fell over his eyes. Eyes of the purest, most stunning blue. Vivid and magnetic, they looked like a blue created by an artist, as if they could never be real.

He looked a great deal like Anthony. But the new earl was more grizzled, his features sharper and more intense. His nose had a bit of a kink to it, as if it had once been broken.

The entire room had gone silent, staring at him in shock and horror. As if a bear had wandered into the drawing room.

For a fleeting moment, Julia saw the American's expression change. The confident smile vanished and a look of hard anger came to his eyes.

Was this evidence of his bitterness? Or perhaps these were all the clothes he had and their shock had hurt him.

Julia helped the countess down to the settee, next to her grandmother.

Then she realized the silence had stretched from awkward to insulting.

No one seemed to know what to do with the earl—Cal—so she smiled at him and stepped forward. She curtsied. "How delightful to have you arrive and I do hope your journey was not too taxing. Shall I have one of the footmen show you to your bedchamber so you can change for dinner? Perhaps you would care to freshen up."

Stubble graced his jaw, as if he had not shaved for days.

Up close, she saw how different he looked from Anthony. He looked too challenging, too bold.

At her small speech of welcome, his golden brows lifted. "My journey wasn't 'taxing' as you put it. I know you aren't the countess. Are you one of my cousins?"

"No, I am a friend of the family. We are neighbors. I am Julia Hazelton. I was engaged to be married to Anthony, who was your cousin, but Anthony was killed at the Somme." She rushed through that bit, giving herself no time to dwell on the words. "Allow me to do the introductions—and if there's a name you forget, don't hesitate to ask."

"Aren't you the sweetheart, Julia?"

The countess made a horrible pained sound. Julia heard her grandmother, the Dowager Duchess of Langford, sputter in outrage.

The mocking tone in his voice made her wary, but she made the introductions of all those in the room. The eligible bachelors had not yet arrived, so it was just the Carstairs family—the countess, Diana and the two other daughters, Cassia and Thalia. And Julia's family.

Zoe greeted Cal with open American charm, welcoming him. Nigel accepted his handshake. Her mother and Grandmama threw looks of sympathy toward the Countess of Worthington. Diana and her younger sisters curtsied.

Julia struggled to not stare at Diana's waist beneath her gold dress. She feared if she did, everyone would read her mind and know her friend's secret. It might be 1925, but to bear a child out of marriage meant a woman was ruined forever.

Would Diana really marry Cal and keep her secret? Julia turned her gaze to Cal. Would her friend really marry him on such an enormous lie?

Goodness, she had looked at him for far longer than was

polite—and he was staring right back at her. With anger crackling in his blue eyes. She smiled calmly at him, though inside her stomach fluttered with shock.

She had grown up around Englishmen—they either showed no emotion at all or they clumsily displayed it. But the energy and emotion—and fury—that seemed to sizzle around this man stunned her.

Was Lady Worthington right? Did he mean to hurt them? Julia would never stand for that. She simply wouldn't.

He still held her gaze. "I'd better go and get dressed," he said.

Wiggins, the butler, moved close to him. "If you need to avail yourself of evening dress, I do believe there are clothes belonging to the late earl that would fit you—"

"I don't need them. I've got my own sets of fancy duds." The anger seemed to abate. His unhurried, naughty grin dazzled again. "I like dressing like this, because I don't need to impress anyone with what I wear. I don't judge a man by his suit. I judge him by his actions."

Julia saw her grandmother lift her lorgnette. "Appropriate dress is an action," the dowager pointed out haughtily.

"I suppose it is." Cal turned his stunning smile onto Grandmama. "But I know how to clean up when I want to."

Then he was gone. Julia's heart was pounding. For some reason, the man set her pulse racing.

"He is awful, isn't he?"

The whisper by her ear startled her. Diana stood at her side, and bit her lip. "He's so rough and uncouth and common. I don't want to marry him, but at the same time...I can't help wanting him."

"Wanting him?" Julia echoed, confused.

"You know...in bed."

"Diana!" Julia exclaimed in a horrified whisper.

2

The American's Revenge

As the butler led him to his bedroom, Calvin Urqhart Patrick Carstairs—now the 7th Earl of Worthington—remembered the shock on Lady Worthington's face when he walked into the drawing room and grinned.

A month ago, he had been woken from a hangover, hauled out of his bed in his apartment in Paris and told by a pale, nervous young lawyer named Smithson that he had inherited a title, three estates and the contents of four modestly invested bank accounts from the family who thought he wasn't good enough to lick their boots.

The lawyer who tracked him down had stammered and blushed throughout the meeting. Cal's latest model, Simone, had been walking around the room half-naked. She liked to feel sunlight pouring through the window on her bare breasts, and she liked to keep Cal looking at her. The lawyer had looked like his eyes were going to leap out of his head.

Cal had poured himself a glass of red wine to clear the hangover, then he'd let the lawyer explain his supposed good fortune—

"The master's apartments have been prepared, my lord."

The snooty tones of the Worthington butler brought Cal back to the present. The man had his hand on the doorknob of the room, but wasn't opening it. Maybe he hoped to learn it was all a joke before he let Cal across the threshold of the earl's bedroom.

It was a double door, so Cal shoved the other door open and walked in.

His trunk and his case were already in the room. The butler pointed out the bed, probably assuming he had no idea what a bed looked like if it wasn't a dirty mattress on the floor. The man opened the doors to the bathing room and the dressing room, as well as a small room with large windows where the earl would traditionally retire to prepare his correspondence.

"It'll do," Cal said indifferently.

Haughtily, the butler tried to look down his nose at Cal—though his eyes came up to Cal's shoulders. "Is your manservant traveling with you?"

"Don't have one," Cal replied, and he laughed at the look of smug satisfaction on the butler's face. "I'm bohemian. Wild and uncivilized. If you think you've been proven right about me because I don't have a valet, wait until I start holding orgies in the ballroom."

The butler turned several fascinating colors. His cheeks went vermilion, his forehead was puce and he developed an intriguing blend of violet and scarlet on his neck.

It gave Cal the itch to create a modernist portrait of an English butler, done in severe blocks of color. Red, purple, yellow-green and stark white.

"When should I tell the countess you will return downstairs?" the man asked, sounding as if his windpipe wasn't drawing air. "I will send a footman to unpack."

"I won't stay up here long. The footman can finish that job while I'm at dinner."

"Very good."

The butler turned away and stalked toward the door, but before he reached it, Cal called, "Wait."

The man turned, lifting his brow self-importantly.

"The dark-haired woman with the pretty blue eyes—Julia Hazelton. Was she really my cousin's fiancée? Anthony died at the Somme, isn't that so?"

"Yes. We lost Lord Anthony to that battle. Indeed, Lady Julia Hazelton was his intended. It was a tragedy, devastating to us all."

Yeah, Cal imagined it would be, since he was standing here now. "Why is she here?"

"Her family was invited to dine, and she is a close friend of the family."

"Did she find someone else—after my cousin died?"

"Lady Julia is still unmarried, my lord. If I may ask, what is the purpose to these questions, my lord?"

"I'm curious," he answered easily. "And if you're going to ask a question anyway, don't waste time asking permission to do it."

The butler, whatever the hell his name was, glared snootily. "Very good, my lord." Bowing, he retreated.

The door closed behind the butler's stiff arse.

For the hell of it, Cal jumped on the bed, landing on his arse in his dusty trousers. He crossed his ankles, his boots on the bed.

He could just hear how his mother would berate him for that, so he slid off.

He went into the bathroom to wash and shave. Showing up scruffy had been his plan and it had served its purpose. The Countess of Worthington, his aunt, had looked like she was going to faint. She would expect him to show up at dinner looking equally bohemian and she would expect that he would have the table manners of an orangutan.

His family had stared at him with suspicion. He'd seen condescension on the countess's face, resentment on the faces of his cousins. His family had all glared at him, sullen, angry…and scared.

Lady Julia had been the only one to welcome him. She had been the perfect English lady to him, polite and unflustered.

Traits he should have hated, given how he knew the aristocracy really behaved. She was likely no different than the rest of them. Masking her disdain behind a polite, reserved smile.

But she had been nice to him. And his mother would say that she didn't deserve to have him judge her—and dislike her—just because of who she was.

Cal opened the bag that contained his straight razor and he filled the small sink with some water—

Hell. That was freezing cold. He ran the other tap, but it didn't get any warmer. Cold-water shaving it would have to be.

He drew the sharp blade along his cheek, slicing off dark blond stubble. He had been looking forward to this ever since that morning when he'd been drinking while the lawyer was outlining the meaning of his new position.

At first he'd wanted to tell the young lawyer with the slicked-back hair to go back to the damned countess and tell her where she and her snobby family could stick their title.

They had disowned his father; they had rejected and vilified his mother for the sin of being an honest, decent woman from a poor family. His mother, Molly Brody, had gone into service to a rich family on Fifth Avenue; his father had been a guest. The usual story. Except his father, Lawrence Carstairs, had been idealistic. He'd fallen in love with the maid he seduced and married her.

Then his father had died. And his mother had gotten sick…

Cal had been fourteen years of age, with a younger brother who was eleven. That was the only reason he'd swallowed his pride and begged the damn Carstairs family for help. He'd been a desperate boy trying to save his mother's life. And they'd refused. To them, he and his mother and his brother, David, didn't exist.

Clearing his throat, the young lawyer had asked him when he would like to book passage back to England.

Cal had been ready to laugh in the face of Smithson Jr. of Smithson, Landers, Kendrick and Smithson. Go to England? He liked painting. He liked Paris. He'd finally found a place where he felt he belonged. He was happy in Paris whether he was sober or drunk, which he felt was a hell of an accomplishment.

"When you take up residence at Worthington Park, there is a dower house available for the countess," Smithson had explained, after pulling at his tie. Simone had come into the kitchen and stood in front of the window so the sunlight limned her naked breasts. Blushing, the lawyer had said, "Should I relay your instruction to have it made ready?"

"For what?" he'd asked.

"For the countess to move into, when you take up residence in your new home."

At that moment, Cal got it. He understood what he'd just been given.

Power.

Now, Cal sloshed the blade in the water and shaved the other side of his face. He patted his skin with a wet cloth, then slapped on some witch hazel. He got dressed in his tuxedo, tied the white bow tie, put on his best shined shoes.

From his trunk, he took out a faded snapshot. It was seven years old. He didn't know why he'd brought it with him. He should have burned it a long time ago. It was a picture of a pretty girl with yellow-blond hair and a sweet face. Her name was Alice and she had nursed him when his plane had been shot down in France. His brother, David, had ended up in the same hospital, three days after Cal got there.

Alice had taken care of David when both of his legs had to be amputated below the knee. Cal had fallen in love with her. The problem was David fell in love with her, too, but without his legs, he wouldn't propose to Alice. And with his brother being in love with her, Cal wouldn't propose, either.

Cal tucked Alice's photograph into the corner of the dressing table mirror.

David had wanted to come here, too. He supposed David had a right to see the house their father had grown up in. He would bring his brother over from America.

The problem was, David was a forgiving kind of man. He was a stronger man than Cal. David wasn't going to like what he planned to do.

But Worthington Park was Cal's chance at revenge.

The Countess of Worthington was shaking. Julia had only seen the countess like this twice—when the telegram had come with its cold, direct message that Anthony had been killed, and the day John Carstairs, her second son, had died in an automobile accident.

"You must have a sherry. Or a brandy. You look very ill." She looked up to summon a drink, but Wiggins was already there. The butler must have almost run at undignified speed to return, and he now presented a delicate glass of sherry on his silver salver.

The countess stared blankly at it, as if she didn't know what to do. Julia took the drink and pressed it into Lady Worthington's hand. The countess's pallor terrified her. She looked more gray than white and quite severely ill.

Julia felt panicked—Lady Worthington had been very ill after Anthony's death. No one had known how to bring her out of grief. Julia had tried very hard to do it. She'd promised Anthony she'd be there for his mother and sisters should anything happen to him, and she always kept her promises.

"The boy is going to destroy us," Lady Worthington moaned.

"He is going to do no such thing," Julia said firmly. She would not allow it. Her mother, Zoe, Nigel and Isobel were conversing with Diana and her younger sisters. The younger ones kept glancing over, looking nervous and curious.

"Have the drink, Sophia," Grandmama insisted. "You will need it."

At Grandmama's firm words, Lady Worthington suddenly took a long sip. "I know what he is going to do," she whispered. "He wrote a letter."

"A letter? What did it say?" Julia asked.

"He threatened us. Simply because he had asked for money and we had the good sense to refuse him. His mother was a grasping, scheming creature. She is the reason my husband's younger brother is dead."

"Goodness, what happened?" Julia asked. "What did she do?"

The countess put her hand to her throat, to rest on the large diamond that sat there. At fifty, the countess wore a fashionable gown—blue silk with a loose, dropped waist, covered in thousands of tiny turquoise and indigo beads.

The Worthington diamonds—huge, heavy and square-cut—glittered on her chest. "I can't speak about it. It is enough to know he is a danger." The countess grasped Julia's hand. "You must not listen to a word he says."

But the plea made Julia uneasy. She remembered Diana's words—that the countess had reason to feel guilty. But the look in the woman's eyes was pure terror. "What is it that you fear he will say?"

"He will tell you lies! Everything that boy says will be twisted and untrue. He will try to make you believe—" Lady Worthington stopped. Her hand clutched the center diamond of her necklace, as if clinging to it gave her strength. "That is not important. You, Julia, should have loyalty to us. Do not welcome him. Do not show him friendship. He will use you to destroy us. Do not forget that. You must be on our side."

"Of course I am." But the countess's words seemed so… extreme. Surely the countess was too upset to go into dinner. Excuses could be made. Julia leaned toward her grandmother. "Perhaps I could take her upstairs—"

"No," the countess cried. "I will not run and hide from Calvin Carstairs. I will protect my family from him. When you have children, you will understand…you would do anything on earth to keep them safe."

And Julia understood. The countess had lost both her sons. She would not allow anyone to hurt her daughters.

"As soon as the boy is downstairs, we will go in for dinner." The countess lifted her chin. Julia was amazed by the woman's strength and spirit.

Until the countess directed a sharp gaze at Diana, standing across the room. "Sometimes you must do something rather terrible to protect those you love."

Julia didn't understand. She had never seen the Countess of Worthington like this. Lady Worthington was usually so gracious, so kind. The tragedy she'd suffered in losing both her sons had broken the hearts of people on the estate, for she was so well loved. When Julia had lost her brother Will to the influenza outbreak and her own mother had sunk deeply into depression, Lady Worthington had been like a mother to her and Isobel.

She had never dreamed Lady Worthington would push anyone into marriage—despite Diana's warning that her mother would scheme to do it. She had thought Diana was exaggerating. Diana had always been dramatic. They had been such opposites—it was why they had always been great friends. "You can't mean to force Diana into marriage—"

"I will do what must be done."

"But not that. You cannot force Diana to be unhappy for the rest of her life—"

"Better that than poverty. Julia, this is not your concern."

The sharp words stung. But the raw fear in her ladyship's eyes startled her.

Yet it was wrong that both the countess and Diana wanted this marriage—it would be a disaster. It was something she felt she could not allow to happen, because it would only cause pain.

Yet, how did she stop it? It might be true that she had no right to interfere, but she also couldn't stand aside and watch a disaster unfurl—

Wiggins's stentorian voice suddenly cut over all sound. "The Earl of Worthington."

From where she stood, Julia could see the entrance to the drawing room. The new earl stood in the doorway…

Tall and broad-shouldered, he wore an immaculate tuxedo jacket, black trousers and white tie. His hair was slicked back neatly with pomade, which darkened it to a rich amber-gold. The severe hair brought out the handsome shape of his jaw, the striking lines of cheekbones you could cut yourself on. Even from across the room, the brilliant blue of his eyes was arresting.

Beside her, a feminine voice drawled, "He was right—he *does* clean up rather well." Diana had moved beside her, perhaps sensing her mother's sharp glance. But Diana set down her empty glass then glided across the drawing room toward her cousin.

Julia had put out her hand instinctively to stop her friend. But she was too late. And what could she do?

She didn't know how to be there for Diana. To be pregnant and unmarried was a nightmare.

Diana's silvery laugh sliced through the room. She was right at the new earl's side, smiling into his eyes, running her strings of glittering jet beads through her fingers. Flirting for all she was worth.

"What's wrong, Julia?"

Zoe, looking lovely in a beaded dress of deep green with an emerald-and-diamond choker around her slim neck, came to her side.

She couldn't talk about Diana's secret, not even to Zoe. She smoothed her face into a look of ladylike placidity. "It's nothing."

"Do you really think Cal is the vengeful monster the countess paints him to be?"

"I don't know."

"It's not stopping the countess from pushing her daughters at him," Zoe observed.

Julia watched Diana move so close to Cal her bosom pressed to his bicep. Cassia, tall and blonde like Diana, but only twenty-one, had approached him, too. She smiled demurely at him—Cassia was always gentle and sweet. The youngest daughter was Thalia: eighteen and bookish. And when Thalia looked as if she wanted to escape, her mother propelled her to talk to Cal.

Then Julia realized Cal was watching Lady Worthington. Just for a moment, then Diana ran her finger along his sleeve and got his attention again.

But Julia had seen the cold, hard rage that seethed in that one fast look.

"I think the countess might be right," Julia said softly.

Zoe looked at her surprised.

Wiggins stepped in the drawing room and cleared his throat. "May I announce His Grace, the Duke of Bradstock. His lordship, the Earl of Summerhay. His lordship, Viscount Yorkville."

Nigel immediately moved to greet his good friend Summerhay.

"Oh no." Julia swallowed hard. At least it would be easy to keep track of the three of them—Bradstock had black hair, Summerhay was blond, Yorkville had auburn waves. Other people arrived also—members of the local gentry, and an older gentleman to make appropriate numbers.

"Don't worry. I'm on your side," Zoe promised. "I don't think you should marry a man you don't love for his title."

It wasn't the right time to speak of it, but Julia suddenly felt she needed to take charge of something. "Zoe, I want to ask if you would consider lending me money."

Her sister-in-law stared in surprise. "Whatever for, Julia?"

"For war widows who have been left destitute. I would like to loan money to the women. They will pay me back over time. All they need is a few pounds to start them on the direction of a new and better life. I asked Nigel for a loan against my dowry, but he refused."

"Did he?"

"He thinks my work is too scandalous and it will ruin

my marriage prospects." She couldn't help it—she glanced at Nigel, who was talking to the three peers who'd just arrived. For all she knew, he was pleading with them to propose to her.

"I would be happy to loan you the money, depending on the amount and the terms," Zoe said. "Is there a great chance these women will default?"

Zoe was never foolish. She was smart and shrewd. "I don't think so," Julia said honestly. "But I will start with modest amounts. If a woman defaults, I will be able to repay out of my pin money and my dress allowance."

"Your dress allowance." Zoe shook her head, obviously amused.

"Do you agree with Nigel?"

"I love my husband, but when it comes to what should be considered scandalous for a woman, we never agree. I am happy you are helping these women."

"You don't fear for my marriage prospects?"

"I already know who you should marry. Noble Dr. Dougal Campbell."

"Zoe…" Julia swallowed hard, aware of the sharp jolt of pain in her heart. "He just wrote to tell me he is engaged to someone else. I have lost him forever."

"Then it was not a great loss, Julia, my dear," the dowager duchess declared.

Julia jumped at the firm, autocratic tones of her grandmother. She turned to find the dowager duchess had walked up beside her and looked ready to deliver advice. Julia dearly loved her grandmother, but as Grandmama looked pointedly at the Duke of Bradstock, she swallowed hard.

"It is if Julia and Dr. Campbell were perfect for each other," Zoe pointed out, sipping her drink and toying with her long string of beads.

Her grandmother linked arms and swept her away from Zoe. "Bradstock keeps watching you," Grandmama said bluntly. "Why do you think he has never married? He is waiting for you. You could be a duchess with one simple word. And that word is *yes*. Julia, you must be settled. Where shall you live, if you end up a spinster?"

"Grandmama, I won't say yes to a man just to have his house. There's absolutely no reason I couldn't have a flat in London and have a job—"

She had to stop. Grandmama staggered back with her hand on her heart. "If I find you behind the counter at Selfridges, my dear, it would be the end of me. You wouldn't want that on your conscience, would you?"

"No, and I'm sure you wouldn't want my unhappy marriage on yours," Julia said.

The dowager's brows rose. "Touché."

Cal was seated between the Duchess of Langford and Lady Julia at the long, wide, polished dinner table. His cousin Diana sat near him, talking flirtatiously to the man beside her—another earl—but glancing at him. The dining table would have stuck out both sides of the narrow tenement building he'd grown up in. The walls and floor of the dining room were covered in Italian marble shot with streaks of pink. On the table there was enough silverware and cut-glass crystal to pay a king's ransom, and half the room was covered in gold leaf.

So damned opulent it made anger boil inside him.

Lady Julia turned to him, a lovely smile on her face, and asked, "What do you think of Worthington Park?"

Up close, Lady Julia—sister to the tall, black-haired Duke of Langford—was even more stunning.

Smooth, alabaster skin. Thick, shining black hair. Huge

blue eyes. Her cool, controlled expression fascinated him.
Like nothing could ever upset her. Though once he saw her
looking at Diana and she'd looked real worried. Maybe because Diana was flirting with him.

Once or twice, he'd seen a look of terror on Lady
Worthington's face. That hadn't stopped her pushing her
three daughters at him. His cousins, damn it. English roy-
alty married their cousins, but it seemed like a strange thing
to him.

The countess obviously hoped the backwater hick from
America would be so bowled over by her pretty English
daughters and their jewels and their manners and their ti-
tles—each one was "Lady" something—that he'd kiss the
ground they walked on and jump down on one knee to propose marriage to one of them.

As if that would happen. He would never marry one of
them—one of the aristocracy.

"Looking at this place," he said to Julia, "I can't believe
no one ever chopped the heads off the English aristocracy."

He figured that would stop her trying to converse with
him.

But it didn't. "I can assure you that many members of the
aristocracy have been afraid of that very thing for quite a long
time," she said smoothly. "But it is that fear that can lead to
more justice for people, for better conditions and more de-
cency—if it is pushed in the right direction."

That answer he hadn't expected. "You almost sound like
a socialist."

"Are you one, Worthington?" At his look of surprise, she
added, "That is how you are to be addressed now. By your
title."

"I remember the lawyer telling me something like that.

But having to hear that title is like having a bootheel ground into my heart. I'd prefer you call me Cal."

Her lips parted. God, she had full, luscious lips.

But then, why shouldn't she? She'd never slaved in a factory for fourteen hours a day. Or spent hours over a tub of steaming water, destroying her hands to scrub dishes.

A footman came by, holding a dish of oysters toward him. When Cal had made his money—a fortune that this family knew nothing about—back in the States from bootlegging and other enterprises that he wouldn't talk about, he'd dined in a lot of nice restaurants. He'd liked knowing he could have whatever he wanted, whenever he wanted it. But the amount of food coming out—and going back—shocked him.

"How much food do you people eat at dinner?" This was the third course and they hadn't gotten to anything that looked like meat.

"There will be several courses, especially at a dinner party," Lady Julia said softly. She kept her voice discreet, he noticed. "I expect the Worthington cook, Mrs. Feathers, wants to impress you."

"Why? No one else around here does."

Lady Julia faced him seriously. "The servants all know that their livelihoods depend on you. On whether you are satisfied with them or not."

"They don't need to knock themselves out," he said. "I'm dissatisfied with this on principle."

Her lips parted—damn, he couldn't draw his eyes away from them. He wanted to hear what she would say, but then the duke sitting on the other side of her started talking to her. Not her brother, but the Duke of Bradstock. Black-haired and good-looking, Bradstock talked like he had a stick up his arse and couldn't find a comfortable place on his chair.

"Lady Julia, have you given up that shocking hobby of

yours?" the duke asked. "Or hasn't your brother taken you in hand?"

Julia turned from him to Bradstock.

For some reason Cal felt damned irritated to lose her attention. Julia was the type of snobbish woman he should avoid. But he liked talking to her. And that surprised him.

"I am not in need of being 'taken in hand,'" Julia said.

"He should forbid these forays into the sordid underbelly, Julia," Bradstock went on.

Cal had no idea what they were talking about, but he could tell Julia didn't like what the man was saying.

"I am over twenty-one, James," she said crisply. "If I choose to do charitable work, I do so. When I told you of my work, I did not think you would hold it against me."

"It shows you have a good heart, my dear." The duke laughed. "There's charity, my dear Julia, but surely this is beyond the pale. These women don't want help. They've found a métier that they enjoy."

"These women are starving and they have children to feed. I think what is beyond the pale is that there is no real help for these women. Their husbands were our heroes. And I don't believe they enjoy what they are doing," she said shortly.

Cal grinned. Not such a snob, then. He liked seeing Lady Julia with her blood running hot.

"My dear girl," Bradstock said condescendingly, "we can't just hand out money *en masse*. Times are hard for all of us. This year, I could only put in half the order for the wine cellar at my hunting box. Austerity has hit us all."

"Hate to think you had to live without a bottle of wine," Cal said. "If Julia is helping the widows of servicemen, I think that is pretty damn admirable."

Bradstock glared at him. "A gentleman doesn't use language like that at the dinner table."

"Where I come from a 'gentleman' doesn't tell a woman what to do when she doesn't want him to."

"And I've heard where you came from was some kind of cesspool," sneered the duke. "You must be extremely grateful you were saved from whatever ditch you were in."

"James, please. And Worthington, I do appreciate your support, but there is no need for heated discussion."

So the duke got a "please" out of her and he got told off. "Get used to it, angel," Cal said. "I'm the earl now."

Her eyes widened in shock.

"If the man from the slums of New York agrees with you, my dear, isn't that a sign you are doing the wrong thing?" Bradstock asked, looking down his nose. Cal would sorely love to rearrange that nose on the handsome idiot's face.

"James, stop it. Let's speak of something else. And do remember Worthington is your host."

But Bradstock wouldn't give it up. "If I were your brother, Julia, I should give you a spanking for being so naughty."

Cal didn't like the hot, appraising look in the bastard's eyes. "If you don't leave her alone," he said heatedly, "I would be happy to beat you up."

"Please, Worthington. Don't. He is teasing." Julia's hand touched his wrist. Once, when he'd been working in a factory after the War, before he went back to life with the Five Points Gang, he'd gotten a shock from an electric outlet. The sizzle and tingle that had shot through his arm was nothing like the one that came from her touch.

Hell, she was everything he didn't want. Privileged. Ladylike. Superior.

Except she had a heart and was willing to defend her beliefs. He liked her—and he hadn't expected to like any of them.

All the men at the table—the Duke of Bad Manners,

the Earl of Whatever, Viscount Something—watched Julia. They couldn't take their eyes off her. Which didn't seem to be making the Countess of Worthington too happy.

Just to piss them off, he said loudly to Julia, "You asked me if I like Worthington. For one man to get all this by the accident of his birth is wrong. A man should earn what he gets."

She didn't look shocked. "I can assure you that an earl who runs his estate properly works extremely hard. A responsible earl ensures his estate prospers, cares for his tenants and acts in a just manner. We are not frivolous and we don't spend money lavishly on ourselves off the backs of others."

He looked pointedly at the marble and gilt. "Don't you?"

"Worthington Park would no longer exist if the men before you did that. Anthony's father was one of the best landowners in the country. He was progressive, fair, compassionate. If he had not been, Worthington would have been destroyed by the harsh times that came both before and after the War."

"And you're telling me the tenants are happy to be poor while the earl is rich?"

"The tenants are happy with their treatment. On an estate like this, everyone knows the value of their place."

So damned arrogant. Cal saw red. "I bet that footman over there would rather be sitting at this table than serving it. In America, he could be—if he worked hard and fought for it."

His voice had dropped, low and angry. Lady Julia stiffened in shock.

"Maybe it would be better to keep the riffraff from inheriting," Bradstock sneered. "Stop bothering Julia. You're not fit to clean her boots. Wasn't your mother some servant?"

Damn you. "My mother was a maid who worked in a mansion on Fifth Avenue and my father met her, fell in love with her pretty face and seduced her."

He heard someone's fork clatter to the plate. Anger drove him on.

"My father didn't leave her high and dry when she became pregnant. He married her and got disowned for doing the right thing by her. But he loved her and she loved him. They spent their lives in squalor and as far as the Earl of Worthington was concerned, my mother, my brother and I didn't exist. We could rot in hell. Too bad for all of you that I didn't rot."

For the first time, the countess spoke to him. "Worthington, we do not discuss our private matters at the dinner table."

"Get used to it," he snapped, like he'd said to Julia. "I'm not ashamed to say where I came from. And truth is, I don't give a damn what you want."

The countess went white.

He knew his mother would have been shocked at his behavior. She had struggled to raise him to be honest and decent and good—then he'd had to throw all that away to survive and help his family after his father was killed.

A lot of good it had done. He'd had to do bad things to bring home money for her and his brother, to support them, to make sure his family survived. He'd had to work for the gang who… Hell, it was join them or be beaten to death by them. After all that, Mam had died anyway—

Cal felt everyone's eyes on him. They all looked at him with disgust or anger. Good—there was no point making them like him before he ripped the estate apart and destroyed Worthington Park—destroyed everything they cared about.

After dinner, Lady Worthington approached her. "I am exhausted. Fear is a very draining thing. Julia, my dear, do help me upstairs."

Then Julia saw Lady Worthington look at Diana and frantically move her head to urge Diana to go to the group of gentlemen who were moving toward the drawing room—Cal, along with the duke and the viscount.

Julia knew what the countess was up to—getting her out of the room to give Diana a better chance to pursue the men.

Then Julia saw Nigel was heading toward her, leading the Earl of Summerhay.

And all she wanted to do was escape. She couldn't face making polite conversation with a man who might want to marry her, when she didn't want him. "I would be happy to take you up to your room, Lady Worthington."

But the countess didn't look pleased her plan had worked. She still looked afraid. Deeply afraid.

When they reached the door of the countess's bedroom, Julia knew she must speak her mind. "You must not force one of your daughters into an unhappy marriage. I will not let the new earl destroy Worthington. Or hurt you."

She was again reminded of the promise she'd made Anthony when he had gone away to war, a promise to look after his family if he didn't come back. His family desperately needed help now, and she must live up to that promise.

The countess laughed. A hard, mirthless laugh, just like Diana's, and it shocked Julia just as much. "What can you do, Julia? Accept that you are as powerless in this as I am."

With that, the countess opened the door to her bedroom and her lady's maid quickly came toward her.

When she returned downstairs, Julia did not go to the Oriental drawing room where everyone had gathered. Instead she slipped through the music room and went out to the terrace that looked over the east lawns and the woods.

The other drawing rooms overlooked the ornate gardens and decorative fountains. But Julia had always loved the view of the woods, which were wild and tangled. Ferns grew all around the edge of them, and the shadowy depths looked like a place where you could find faeries if you were very quiet and waited without moving. Julia used to do that with Diana, Cassia and Thalia when they were children.

Later, she would walk through the woods with Anthony. Looking at them brought that poignant mix of emotion, remembered happiness and pain.

Was she powerless to help? Or could she be like Zoe? Be courageous and grasp life. She believed the countess—who had been so kind to her when she was young and her own mother had fallen deeply into grieving—and Diana, her good friend, were worth fighting for.

"Lady Julia."

She knew who stood behind her from the husky male voice with its distinct American twang. She turned, rubbing her arms as a cool breeze rippled over her. "Good evening, Worthington. It's a lovely night."

He came out onto the terrace, his hair almost silver in the bluish moonlight. Shadows made his cheekbones look even more pronounced, revealed a slight cleft in his chin and curved around his full, sensual mouth. He definitely looked wilder, rougher than Anthony had done. Cal looked untamed and by comparison Anthony had looked gentle and domesticated.

Cal grinned at her around an unlit cigarette he had clamped in his teeth. "I saw you sneak past the drawing room to come out here. Escaping your suitors?"

So he'd noticed that. She was surprised. "I just needed a bit of air."

"You're shivering," he observed.

She turned from the balustrade, toward the glass-paned door. "I should go back inside."

"Don't go back in. Here, have this—" In a quick movement, he pulled off his jacket and gallantly draped it around her shoulders. She was wrapped in his warmth, in his masculine scent—slightly smoky and earthy, and crisp with witch hazel.

He held it around her and stepped close to her. "You're different than the rest of them."

Caught in the embrace of his coat, she felt a shiver go down her spine. He looked so much like Anthony, yet he was so utterly different. It was confusing. Her heart raced, and she felt, strangely, on the verge of tears just from looking at him. She couldn't stop gazing at his face, thinking how familiar it was. But this was not Anthony. He wasn't Anthony come back to her. He was someone else.

"You're angry with me still," he said.

"No. I was just…just lost in thought. In memories." Then she thought: she must get to know this man. If she were to do battle with him, she must understand him. "How am I different?" she asked.

"You welcomed me and you don't talk to me like you hate the sight of me. I'm sorry I was rude to you at dinner. You didn't deserve that."

He looked so forlorn, her heart suddenly panged for him.

This didn't sound like an angry, vengeful man. How hard this must be for him, to suddenly become an earl, to be thrust into a position of responsibility, with a family he didn't know.

"You must understand Lady Worthington," she said impulsively. "Women in our situation know someone new will inherit and we could lose our homes. That is why the countess is so sharp. She really is a good person—she was always like a second mother to me. She is simply afraid. If you were to reassure them they have nothing to fear, I am sure it would help."

Cal looked at her thoughtfully. "What's she so afraid of?"

"She fears you will turn her and her daughters out of the house with nothing."

He stepped back from her. From a pocket, he drew out a silver-colored lighter and lit his cigarette. He leaned on the balustrade and smoked, his shoulders hunched and tense.

"The estate is mine now," he said. "I can do whatever I want with it. Maybe she's right to be afraid."

Julia's heart skipped a beat. "What do you mean? What do you mean to do?"

"Maybe exactly what she fears," he said softly.

"What did she do that deserves such a punishment?"

He blew smoke into the dark. Then he said, "I'm gonna sell the other estates—the hunting place, the house in Scotland. As for Worthington Park, I'm gonna sell it piece by piece."

Horror gripped Julia. She stumbled back, gripping his coat. "You can't do that! You can't destroy Worthington!"

"The countess was right. To say I'm bitter and vengeful would be an understatement. I want to torture the Carstairs family with the pain of watching something they love die."

"You cannot do this! Think of the tenants—all the people who live on this estate and rely upon it. What are you going to do with them? This house has been in the Worthington family for four hundred years." She began to tremble. Anthony had loved Worthington Park. He was devoted to keeping it strong and secure. She and Anthony would talk of future plans when they were married—improvements to the house, a new nursery, a garden in which children could play. New equipment for the farm, improvements to the school so all the children of the estate would be educated.

"You can't destroy the estate," she went on, trying to fight the shakiness of her voice. "It would be heartless. Senseless. If you really want revenge, be the most beloved Earl of Worthington there has ever been. Prove them wrong."

He laughed—a hard, bitter laugh. "No one here is ever going to love me. These estates should be ripped apart. They belong to the people. There should be no lords and masters."

Her heart thundered. "Well, there are even in America. Can you tell me that in America, rich men believe poor men are equal to them? You can't, I'm sure." She leveled him with a firm gaze. "And I will stop you."

He looked amused. "How do you plan to do that, Lady Julia?"

"I will—" She didn't know what she would do but she had to think of something. She couldn't watch Worthington—the place Anthony had loved with all his heart—be destroyed. "I will make you understand you have a responsibility to the land, the house and the people who live on the estate. I won't stop until you love Worthington so deeply, you won't let it go because it is a part of your soul."

"That'll never happen."

"Yes, it will." She pulled his tailored tuxedo jacket off her shoulders and shoved it at him.

He caught it and straightened, towering over her. A roguish smile curved his lips. "We'd better go back inside, Lady Julia. Even I know that if we're away from the crowd long enough, people are gonna start talking about us."

He took out the cigarette. His mouth lowered toward hers.

She was literally shaking in her shoes. Shaking with fury. But also with something else. With heat and confusion and a sudden, intense...*whoosh*.

Dear God, she wanted to kiss him.

And he was awful. Cruel. The enemy.

She took a determined step back and glared at him. "If you think I would kiss you after you just announced you would destroy this beautiful place and ruin hundreds of people's lives, you are mad. Nothing is going to happen between us. Not *ever*."

She turned and walked toward the door, determined not to shiver in the cool night air.

"I think you're wrong," he called out behind her.

She turned. In clear, no-nonsense tones, she said, "The only thing that will happen between us is that I will make you see sense, Worthington."

She had no idea just how to do that at the moment, but it made a rather lovely exit line. Julia tipped up her chin and went inside, for once thankful she had been trained with a book on her head and could glide in victorious manner with aplomb.

3

Two Proposals of Marriage

Julia stormed back toward the drawing room.

How could she have felt a sudden, dizzying *whoosh* for *that* man?

The *whoosh* had been something she'd experienced with Anthony—that sudden feeling of the world stopping on its trajectory, while she looked into his eyes as if for the very first time.

She'd felt it with Dougal Campbell within minutes of meeting him. It had been when he had begun to describe the surgery he had performed to repair a child's leg and save it from amputation. Her head had swum a little at the thought of an operation, but she had fallen in love with him right then, right there, because he had been so passionate about what he'd done.

Dougal—well, she'd lost Dougal forever now. He was marrying the daughter of a doctor, a girl who would make the perfect doctor's wife. She was happy for him—he deserved the perfect wife.

But after caring so deeply for Dougal, how could she have had that devastating moment of—of something with Cal?

He actually thought he could kiss her *after* what he'd threatened to do to Worthington. Well, really! And she now knew why she had been riveted to the spot, unable to move. She had been shocked. That was all.

The man was infuriating. Not because he was angry and hurting—she could understand that, if his family had been rejected by the previous earl. His father had been disowned after all.

No, he was infuriating because his mind was closed. This was the modern world—every breath you took was full of change. He must let the past go.

Destroying something never fixed anything. Heaping on more pain never made pain go away. She was certain of it. *Healing* was the most important thing in the world. Zoe had healed Nigel, helping him finally escape the way the War had hurt him. Her mother needed to heal more from the grief of losing Will—if Mother could, she could be happier.

Julia knew the power of healing. She had to make Cal see it.

"Julia."

She almost collided with the Duke of Bradstock as he stepped out of the shadows.

Frowning, he looked down at her. "You were outside with that American, Julia. I saw him follow you out onto the terrace. Did you invite him out there?" he demanded.

James had followed her. Why? Because Cal had?

"I went out on the terrace for some air," she said. "Then the new earl joined me."

"So he just followed you." James grasped her wrist and held it in the circle of his long, strong fingers, capturing her. He peered at her face in the darkness of the corridor—only two electric lights illuminated it. "You look upset. Did he try to force himself on you? Tell me and I'll grind him under my heel like the piece of dirt he is."

Most girls thought the Duke of Bradstock was more handsome than any movie star in the pictures. His features were striking and autocratic; his hair raven black, his eyes dark green and surrounded by thick, long lashes. He had a wicked allure, like Valentino.

Grandmama believed he was interested in Julia, since he had never married after he returned from the War. Grandmama's words haunted her: *you could be a duchess with one simple word.*

James was looking at her...as if he would slay a dragon if she asked.

For some reason, she did not feel like a heroine who wished to swoon into the muscular arms of a sheikh-costumed Valentino. She was angry with Cal, but she would not insult him. "He is not a piece of dirt—he is the Earl of Worthington, and we are in his house, James. It is most impolite to be rude. And we simply spoke out on the terrace. Worthington was the perfect gentleman."

"Was he? You were trembling when you came back inside."

"It was cold outdoors."

"I saw his face when he was looking at the countess across the dinner table. Pure hatred. What reason does he have to hate them?"

"That is the mystery, isn't it? I don't know. But I really must find out, if I am to fix this problem and put a stop to Cal's plans."

"Cal? You call him Cal? What plans?"

"He objects to Worthington," she said, not quite answering his questions.

"My God, Julia, you can't approve of this upstart and his lack of manners and breeding?"

What an odd question. She should disapprove of Cal—of everything he intended to do and the way in which he meant to do it. But she knew about grief and pain, how viciously it could hurt.

James moved closer. Suddenly, he clasped her hand in both of his large ones. "Julia—" His voice was husky. "Julia, you must know how I feel about you."

Oh…oh heavens. Grandmama was always right. It was an idiotic thought, but the very first one that leaped into her mind.

"I had no choice but to let you go to Anthony Carstairs," he continued. "You were so fond of him, and he was a friend of mine. Then, after his death, I waited patiently. It has been nine years. Julia, I want to marry you. I must marry you."

Oh heavens. She did not love this man. She'd known him since he was a boy and he had only ever been interested in one thing—himself. And if she were his wife, she could never do anything unless he gave her permission. That was the kind of marriage that existed decades ago. It was one she would never accept.

Grandmama would faint when she learned what her granddaughter was going to do. Gently Julia said, "James, I am so very flattered by your proposal. I am so sorry you've waited for so long—"

"Don't go on," he said brusquely. "There is no need." He released her hand and stepped back. His face became a hard, emotionless mask. "But I would like to know why."

"It is not you. Truly, it isn't. I just—I just am filled with thoughts of Anthony still." But there had been Dougal, so she knew her heart could be touched. Just not by this man.

"Even after this long? Julia, I would treat you like a queen. You would reign over my four estates. I still have a considerable income. My God, Julia, I dream of you every night."

He grasped her wrist again, this time hard enough that she winced.

"James, you are hurting me."

"I'm sorry." He released her. "I've been a damned fool, haven't I?" he said harshly. "Hoping you might realize how much I want you to be my duchess."

He looked at her with such hurt she felt guilty. But she'd never asked him to hope or wait. Never once had she been anything beyond polite and proper.

But this was going to turn messy and emotional and unpleasant, and all her training leaped to the fore. "Dear James, any woman would jump at your proposal. But you deserve a woman who can give you her entire heart. I can't."

"But if you could—" He left the sentence hanging.

What did she do? Lie? It was the ladylike thing to do. One simple statement had her facing the most stunning truth— did she want to be a lady and lie, or did she want to be bold and brave and tell the truth? "If I could...well, things would be quite different, I assure you."

That was a lady's response. It didn't insult and it said absolutely nothing. She felt rather guilty giving it. But her heart told her it was for the best.

"Julia, I can't wait any longer."

"I don't want you to wait, James. Please, do find someone else and be happy."

He straightened his dinner jacket. "I bid you good-night then."

He was gone.

Julia let out a deep, relieved breath.

Then she heard a soft movement. Smoke drifted out from the doorway of the music room. She suspected Cal was in there. He must have come in from the terrace and heard everything. She stalked to the door. Cal was leaning against the fireplace mantel.

He looked up as she walked in. "Why did you refuse him?"

Julia felt her cheeks get hot. "That is none of your business."

"He's a duke, isn't it? Your family's gonna be disappointed."

"My family accepts that I will marry only for love."

"That's what you want? Love? Love can destroy you, you know. It can hurt you like nothing else can."

And he had been hurt. Very badly. By the loss of his parents? Or by something else? "I know that," she said softly. "I lost my fiancé. I know how much it can hurt to love someone and lose them."

"Do you think it's worth it?" he said suddenly.

"Of course it is."

"I disagree."

"Tell me why your heart is so badly broken," she said impulsively.

But he only grinned. "Angel, I have no heart to break." He threw the stub of his cigarette into the fireplace grate and, this time, he walked away from her.

Of course, it was because he was running away from her question.

In the kitchen of Worthington Park, early in the morning, Hannah Talbot let out a huffing breath as she lifted the porridge dish. This was the plain one, the one used for the servants' dinners and not one of the large gleaming silver dishes that was kept under lock and key. That one she never had to clean. As kitchen maid, she was too lowly. The butler, Mr. Wiggins, and the footmen tended to the silver.

With Tansy, the new girl, pretending to be sick this morning, Hannah had done the work of two maids. Her arms ached from polishing the range until it shone like a mirror. She'd had to lay the fires in all the rooms, make the morning tea, as well as stir three pots of sauce at once, since Tansy wasn't there to do any of it.

And she'd had to do it perfectly. With the new earl arriving, Mrs. Feathers, the cook, was in a state. She'd snapped at Hannah for making mistakes when Hannah had been doing the work of two women at once!

Then, while rushing through laying the fires, Hannah had gone to check on Tansy, only to find their room empty!

Tansy wasn't sick at all. She'd gone sneaking off somewhere.

Hannah could have told Mrs. Feathers. But maybe there had been an emergency and Tansy had been too afraid to ask if she could have the morning off. Tansy had a large family and there was always someone sick or having a baby. Hannah had no family anymore. While Tansy complained about having a huge family who were always telling her what to do, Hannah envied her.

The other servants were already seated at the table as she hefted the pot into the servants' dining hall and set it on the table. Mrs. Feathers waited with the ladle and porcelain bowls. "What were you doing, girl? Harvesting the grain yourself?"

"I'm sorry," Hannah set the pot down as carefully as she could.

The maids and footmen, the valet, her ladyship's lady's maid, the daughters' lady's maid, the housekeeper and Mr. Wiggins sat around the table with their tea or coffee before them. Hannah always had to make tea for everyone else—

it was hours after she awoke that she got anything. She was dying for a cuppa, but she had to fetch the other food first.

Finally she was able to slip into the only empty chair with a cup of tea for herself, just as Amy, the new parlor maid who came from London, asked, "What did ye think of him?"

"Who?" Stephen, the senior footman asked.

Hannah's heart gave a little flip-flop in her chest. Stephen had a delicious voice. And he was handsome enough to be a film star, she was sure.

"Rudolph Valentino," Amy said pertly. "His lordship, of course. The new earl."

"He's handsome," Miss White said. Pale and red-haired, she was lady's maid to Ladies Diana, Cassia and Thalia.

"Did you see what he was wearing when he arrived last night? My brother works on a farm and he's better dressed."

"That will be enough, Amy," warned Mrs. Rumpole, Worthington's housekeeper. She always wore a long black dress, and her graying hair was pulled back severely. The maids were terrified of her; Hannah was terrified of Mrs. Feathers, the cook.

"He's got no man of his own," said Mr. St. Germaine, the valet. "So it looks like I'll be dressing him. It's like trying to mold a diamond out of an unformed lump of coal."

Amy giggled at that, flashing her dark eyes at the valet, who was dapper and good-looking, but was apparently quite old because he never looked at the women, not even the young and pretty ones like Amy.

All the maids started talking about the new earl and what they thought of him. Then one asked her, "What do you think of him, Hannah?"

Her cheeks got hot. "I didn't see him. I didn't get lined up for him." She never was presented with the rest of the staff. And the new earl had shown up much later than expected—he'd telephoned to say he would be late. When Mr. Wiggins told him the staff would be presented to him and that the "lineup," as she called it, would delay dinner, the new earl had insisted they not do it. Mr. Wiggins had put it off until this morning.

"Hannah doesn't have time to think about anything but her work," said Mrs. Feathers sharply. "She has to get her breakfast finished. She's got pots to wash. Then we've got to start on the food for luncheon and on the desserts for tonight's dinner. And woe betide us if his lordship isn't pleased with the meals. We'll be out on our beam ends."

Dutifully Hannah finished her porridge. She wished just for once she could relax over a meal and not have to run about like a chicken with her head cut off. But Mrs. Feathers had been unusually worried and snappish ever since the new earl arrived.

She truly wanted to see the new earl—she hated being the only servant here who hadn't done so, due to her lowly rank. She'd hoped he might go into the study or the library while she was making the fires, so she could see him, but no such luck.

After breakfast, she had to plunge her sore hands into steaming hot water to clean the pots and dishes after breakfast. Then Tansy walked in.

"I was feeling much better, Mrs. Feathers, so I thought I would come and help."

"How sweet of you to volunteer your services, Your Highness," said the cook to Tansy. "One would never know that's what you're paid to do. Now hurry up and get to work. Hannah can't handle this lot on her own."

Hannah's cheeks burned. She thought she was doing a magnificent job in coping. When Mrs. Feathers left them, she looked at Tansy, who wasn't getting to work all that quickly. "Where were you? You weren't in bed when I looked."

Tansy, who had wavy black hair and huge blue eyes, paled. "Did you tell her?"

"No, but what happened to you?"

"I went for a drive, Hannah. My gentleman took me for a drive in his beautiful car."

"In the morning?"

"It was the only time he could come, and I knew I could slip out if I said I were sick."

"So you went alone with him in his car?"

Tansy gave a wicked smile. "I did. He drove us out to Lilac Farm and we parked under the trees. He kissed me!"

"Is that all he did?"

"He's a gentleman. A real gentleman. He said he knows he can't expect more unless he marries me. I can tell he wants me. He's going to propose. He's so much in love with me."

Hannah sighed. "But he's a gentleman and you're a kitchen maid."

"But I am pretty—I'm not being immodest. He says I could be a film star. And he's got scads of money. He's got that lovely motor car, and he's been ever so generous with me. I don't think he cares that I'm only a scullery maid."

"All gentlemen care."

"That's not true. They do marry girls from trade."

"That's because those girls have enormous dowries."

Tansy folded her arms over her chest. "Look at the new earl. If a man who was nobody can become an earl, I believe it is possible to better yourself."

Hannah rolled her eyes. "He's the earl because his father was the old earl's brother, silly goose. Since girls can't inherit, and you don't have an earl in your family tree, you have no hope of joining those upstairs."

"I will if I marry a gentleman. And the earl's father married a maid—I heard the story."

"That's one story with a happy ending. Most of the time, gentlemen don't marry the likes of us."

"That they don't!" Mrs. Feathers's booming voice made both her and Tansy jump. "If I catch you flirting with any gentlemen, you'll be out of here without a reference. I'll not keep a girl around who's determined to get herself into trouble! Now, stop your woolgathering, the both of you, because if your sauces are not more than a charred coating on the bottom of a pot, you'll both be gone! And you'll have my boot in your backsides to send you on your way."

Tansy quickly grasped a spoon and stirred hurriedly.

Hannah stirred, too. She didn't say a word but tears stung her eyes. She had not done a thing wrong. Not one thing. Tansy was the one who caused trouble, but her trouble always seemed to include Hannah.

The youngest footman, Eustace, burst in, out of breath. He ran right into the table and Hannah had to sweep her bowl into her arms to keep it safe.

"What demon is chasing you?" Mrs. Feathers demanded.

"His lordship is downstairs," Eustace managed to gasp, between sucking in deep breaths. "Said he wants to talk to you, Mrs. Feathers."

"For pity's sake, what does he want? If he wants a proper dinner, he should be leaving me alone to get it ready."

But for all Mrs. Feathers spoke in her usual sharp, impatient tones, Hannah saw she looked dreadfully worried.

At Brideswell Abbey, Julia went down to breakfast early. In the dining room, the warming dishes were out on the sideboard and the coffee urn was set up, but the room was empty.

She'd feared Nigel would be waiting, ready to propel the

Earl of Summerhay at her. Or her mother would have heard, somehow, that she'd refused a duke, and would be ready to lecture her. Mother continually pointed out that one thing had not changed in the modern world—men still wanted young brides and Julia was going to end up on the shelf.

Julia filled her plate and carried it to the table, when a low, deep voice said, "G-good morning, Lady Julia."

She turned and faced the Earl of Summerhay. Who wore riding clothes. And a slight blush.

"Good morning. I take it you are riding today? It's the perfect day for it—not too hot yet," she said brightly. Weather was the safest and most mundane of topics.

Last night, she had spoken to him a little at Worthington Park, and then at Brideswell, after they'd returned and before they had gone up to bed.

Nigel had tried to encourage him to talk about the heroic things he'd done in the War. But he had been very modest about all that. Nigel told her Summerhay had saved many men's lives. He had captured a German machine gun nest single-handed. He was indeed a hero—a quiet and unassuming one.

She liked that about him.

But there hadn't been any moment with him when the world had halted on its axis. She didn't know why not—it simply hadn't.

In fact, she had rejoined the group after James's proposal. She had been talking to Summerhay when Cal had entered the drawing room. For a moment, she didn't hear anything poor Summerhay was saying.

Of course, that was because she'd been afraid of what Cal was going to do. Mysteriously, he hadn't done anything at all. He hadn't caused a scene or made any threats. He had played the perfect host. And she couldn't understand why—

"Yes, I'm going riding with Nigel," Summerhay said. "Care to join us?"

He looked so hopeful, her heart ached. "I would have loved to, but I have commitments for the morning. I rode earlier."

"I'm too late, then." He looked rueful. "I've heard you're a bally good rider. Nigel admits you've bested him at some fences. That's high praise since he never likes to admit he's been beaten."

She smiled. "Marriage changed my brother quite a lot." Then she could have bitten off her tongue. Talking about marriage was not a good idea.

"He's a lucky man to have found such a lovely wife. I hope to be as fortunate." Then suddenly, earnestly, he said, "Julia, I would like to see more of you. You are one of the most remarkable women I've ever met."

Oh dear. She was not on the shelf yet apparently.

Summerhay was a nice and charming man. For one moment, she thought: *This might be my last chance to marry. And he is a good man.*

"Julia—?" He was brilliant red now, the Earl of Summerhay. "I know we have barely spent time together but I am hoping…hoping that when we know each other better, you might consider doing me the honor of… No, I'm sorry. It must be too early for that for you. But I know my own heart."

Could love and desire grow? Did love have to be instantaneous?

But she thought of walking down the aisle and saying "I do" and not being in love with him. She couldn't do it. And it would be wrong to do it to a hero.

"I do enjoy your company, but my charitable work is taking up almost all of my time." That was too obviously an excuse. This man deserved honesty. For she could spend time with him, let him court her, but when she searched her heart, she didn't want to. It was wrong to judge so quickly, but she thought of being courted and she wanted to…to run, really.

"The truth is, I had already given my heart to a doctor," she explained, "but he has gone to London to work at a hospital. I know it takes me a long time to get over a lost love. I mean this as no slight against you. I am just not ready to move on."

"But you will be—someday?"

"I don't know," she said truthfully. "And so I can't ask you to wait."

"I want to wait."

"No, please. I can't make you any promises, Summerhay."

"I know that. If I wait, that's on my conscience, not yours. It's a chance I am willing to take." He stood, bowed. "I should go and prepare for riding. Until later."

Then he was gone.

She knew in her heart she had done the right thing. She wanted the *whoosh*. Even if it meant no marriage at all. Which meant she'd best be prepared to make a life without a wedding.

On the way out of the dining room, she encountered Zoe, who smiled and said, "I've decided that your plan to help your war widows is sound. You don't need to worry about taking a loan against your dowry. We'll be partners. I'll provide the financial backing and business advice, you will work with the widows to help them create businesses that are suitable."

She threw her arms around Zoe, who laughed. "I've never seen you look so bubbly, Julia."

"I don't know if I've ever been quite so happy. Except when you married Nigel. Good things will come of this, Zoe. I feel I am about to change the world." Or at least her precious corner of it.

4

Modern Art

Julia knew of one thing that could make a woman forget about marriage and love and all its associated problems.

Well, two things.

She left the house, walking briskly to Brideswell's garage. She had money thanks to Zoe. And a list of women whose lives she was about to change.

That was the first thing that was more important than suitors and marriage.

The second?

Her beloved automobile—a brand-new roadster from America with glossy paint and shiny chrome, leather seats, leather-wrapped steering wheel and an engine that roared with power.

She was driving past the house, toward the front gate, when a young footman ran out and stopped her.

Over the rumble of the idling engine, he shouted, "Lady Diana at Worthington Park asked if you might drive over there right away. She says they are in the midst of a disaster and only you can help, milady."

Julia's heart plunged. The new Earl of Worthington—Cal—must have told them his plans. "Thank you, George." She put her motor into gear and pressed on the accelerator. Trixie, her motorcar, roared down the gravel drive and through the open main gates.

When Julia arrived, Diana met her on the drive. "Goodness, you look pale," Julia gasped. "Are you ill? Is this about Cal's—?"

"Not here." Diana dragged her to the music room. Sunlight flooded in on the grand piano, the harp, the cluster of gilt-and-silk chairs. A maid came in with a tray of coffee and before Julia could ask her question, the countess burst in. Her plucked brows flew up in surprise. "Why are you here, Julia—?"

"To see me, Mother," Diana said. "I asked her to come, since you are so upset. Julia will know what to do."

"Yes, I suppose Julia will." Lady Worthington sank into a chair. "Mrs. Feathers has quit! That *man* went down to the kitchens and questioned everything she did. Even suggested the servants should eat better and there should be less waste in the dining room. Apparently he cast some aspersion on her character—she believed he accused her of *theft*. She is packing her bags as we speak. He has done this deliberately to spite us, for where can one find a cook at short notice? He fired his valet, a hall boy and a footman this morning and he has driven away our cook."

Julia stared, dumbfounded. Heavens, Cal had already begun.

"This is wretched," she said. "How can he fire the staff when work is so hard to find?"

"*Servants* are hard to find," Lady Worthington said, holding out her hand gracefully for coffee.

Julia poured and gave the countess a cup, then handed

one to Diana, who looked everywhere but at her mother and tapped her foot anxiously.

"The *earl* declared they should find real work and 'do better,'" the countess cried. "Do better than work at Worthington Park? Preposterous!"

Cal simply didn't understand. Many of the servants didn't want to "do better," which often meant long hours in gruesome conditions in factories and offices. They took pride in their work running a great house.

The countess tried to set down her cup, but her hand shook so badly the cup overturned, spilling coffee. "Blast!" the countess gasped. Then she began to sob, burying her face in her hands. Diana stared helplessly, in shock.

Julia quickly put her arm across the countess's shoulders. "I will see about this, I promise. I will stop him."

"Stop him?" The countess lifted her head from her hands. She had turned a terrible shade of light gray and looked deathly ill. "What do you mean?"

Julia swallowed hard. "Did Cal tell you he intended to do this? Did he speak of any plans he has, now that he is the earl?"

"I do not care what he wants—" Lady Worthington broke off, putting her hands to her mouth. Through them, she cried, "I wish we could be rid of him! But we can't." She turned to Diana. "The only way I can see that we might have some protection is to have influence over him. As his wife, you would exert some control. Go and *find* him."

"Go and find him and do what with him?" Diana protested.

Lady Worthington had been on the verge of collapse. Now she became commanding and strong once more. "We are desperate, Diana. Go at once and make him fall in love with you. It is the only hope we have."

"Mummy, one doesn't just go up to a man, especially a horrible, obstinate, hate-filled man like that, snap her fingers and make him fall in love."

"You've always been a determined flirt, Diana. For heaven's sake, put it to good use for once!"

Diana burst into tears, turned and ran from the room.

"The girl is being an utter fool! Does she not see what will happen to us if she does not do this? She must marry the new earl."

Cal's arrival—and the fear of what he would do—had changed Lady Worthington completely. Julia had never seen her behave cruelly with her daughters. "Diana is just as afraid as you are," Julia said softly. Probably more, she thought. "Please don't be harsh with her."

"I must be harsh, or we're ruined. I suppose she is balking at her duty. She is behaving like a foolish modern girl who wants to marry for love. I suppose she has fallen in love with someone unsuitable, just to spite me."

"How—?"

"Aha! I thought as much." The countess fixed Julia with a penetrating gaze. Julia was astounded at the rapid change in the woman—she had been on the verge of collapse, now she was sharp and angry. This must be what sheer fear did to a person. And it appeared Cal hadn't told her of his plan. Lady Worthington did not know the worst of what Cal wanted to do.

"Who is she in love with?" the countess demanded.

Julia swallowed hard. She believed in honesty but she had to lie for Diana. "You are wrong. She is willing to marry him. For all your sakes."

"Do not sound so disapproving with me, Lady Julia Hazelton. I will protect my family at any cost. Remember that."

"But Cal is in pain, as well," Julia said. "I do not approve